Ramadan

Tatiana Tomljanovic

Weigl Publishers Inc.

Published by Weigl Publishers Inc.
350 5th Avenue, Suite 3304, PMB 6G
New York, NY 10118-0069
Web site: www.weigl.com

Library of Congress Cataloging-in-Publication Data

Tomljanovic, Tatiana.
 Ramadan / Tatiana Tomljanovic.
      p. cm. -- (American holidays)
Includes index.
 ISBN 1-59036-461-9 (hard cover : alk. paper) -- ISBN 1-59036-464-3 (soft cover : alk. paper)
 1. Ramadan--Juvenile literature. 2. Fasts and feasts--Islam--Juvenile literature. I. Title. II. Series: American
holidays (New York, N.Y.)
 BP186.4.T67 2006
 297.3'62--dc22

                                    2006014038

Printed in the United States of America
1 2 3 4 5 6 7 8 9 0 10 09 08 07 06

Editor Heather C. Hudak
Design and Layout Terry Paulhus

Cover A Malay girl reads from the
Muslim holy book, the Qur'an.

All of the Internet URLs given in the book were valid at the time of publication. However, due to the dynamic nature of the Internet, some addresses may have changed, or sites may have ceased to exist since publication. While the author and publisher regret any inconvenience this may cause readers, no responsibility for any such changes can be accepted by either the author or the publisher.

Every reasonable effort has been made to trace ownership and to obtain permission to reprint copyright material. The publishers would be pleased to have any errors or omissions brought to their attention so that they may be corrected in subsequent printings.

Contents

Introduction

★ ★

Muslims fast during Ramadan.

Ramadan is a special month in the Muslim calendar. Muslims are people who follow the religion called Islam. Islam means **"submission"** to the will of Allah. Allah is the supreme being that Muslims worship. During the entire month of Ramadan, Muslims **fast**. They do not eat or drink anything between sunrise and sunset. Muslims fast to show their **devotion** to Allah. They also fast so they know what it is like for people who have little to eat.

Not all Muslims fast during Ramadan. Children under the age of 12 are not expected to fast. Pregnant women, sick people, and people traveling on long journeys are not expected to fast either.

Muslims consider bad behavior to be wrong all of the time, but during Ramadan, behaving badly is considered especially wrong.

The crescent shape of the new moon marks the beginning of Ramadan.

Islam the Religion

★ ★

Muslims believe that there is no God but Allah.

The Islamic faith is based on five rules. These rules are called the five Pillars of Islam. Like a pillar of stone that holds up a building, the five pillars hold up Islam.

- The first rule is the *shahadah*. This means that Muslims believe that there is no God but Allah and that Muhammad is the messenger of Allah.

- The second rule is *salat*. This means "daily prayer." Muslims pray five times a day.

- The third rule is *zakat*. This means "**charity**." It is especially important for Muslims to give to charity during Ramadan.

- The fourth rule is *sawm*. This rule calls for a month of fasting during Ramadan.

- The fifth rule is the *hajj*, or "**pilgrimage**." Muslims must make a pilgrimage to Mecca at least once in their life. Mecca is a holy city in Saudi Arabia.

At the end of their pilgrimage to Mecca in Saudi Arabia, Muslims pray at Mecca's Grand Mosque. A mosque is a holy place of worship for Muslims.

Muhammad the Prophet

Mecca became the most important city in Islam.

Muslims believe that Muhammad is the final **prophet** in Islam. He was born in Mecca in AD 570. Like many men in his family, Muhammad became a trader.

Muhammad devoted himself to religion and called the faith that he taught Islam. Many people in Mecca did not want to follow Muhammad's teachings. For a few years, the Muslims fought battles with the Meccans. Finally, the war ended, and the Muslims entered Mecca peacefully. Mecca became the most important city in Islam. Muhammad died on June 8, 632.

DID YOU KNOW?

Muhammad did not believe that people should be judged by their class, color, or race.

From an early age, young Muslims are encouraged to read the Qur'an, the holy book of Islam.

The Holy Qur'an

★ ★

The Qur'an teaches about Allah.

For Muslims, the Qur'an is the actual word of Allah. Muslims believe that the Angel Gabriel spoke Allah's words into Muhammad's ears. Muhammad repeated exactly what he had been told to people who wrote it down. The word *Qur'an* means "**recitation.**"

Much of the Qur'an is about Allah's relationship with people. The Qur'an teaches about Allah and creation, laws, and how to live a good life. Muslims consider the gift of the Qur'an a **miracle**.

DID YOU KNOW?

The Qur'an should not come into contact with anything dirty. It is never put on the ground.

Muslims believe that they are closest to Allah when they repeat the Qur'an aloud. Both listening to and reciting the Qur'an are considered an act of worship. A person who has memorized the whole Qur'an is known as a *hafiz*, or someone who keeps the Qur'an in their heart. It is a special act of devotion to recite the whole Qur'an at least once during Ramadan.

People can learn about Allah's teachings by reading and memorizing the Qur'an. Muslims begin studying the Qur'an when they are children. The Qur'an is written in Arabic.

Creating the Holiday

Muslims have a festival called Eid al-Fitr.

The first **revelations** came to Muhammad more than 1,400 years ago, during the month of Ramadan. This is why Muslims fast during Ramadan. They show their devotion to Allah by fasting.

To celebrate the end of Ramadan, Muslims have a festival called *Eid al-Fitr*. The first Eid was celebrated in AD 624 by Muhammad and his friends and family. Eid al-Fitr means the "festival of the fast breaking." It begins when the new moon has been spotted at the end of Ramadan. Friends and families gather for big meals.

During Eid al-Fitr, children often receive gifts, such as money or sweets.

Most Muslims believe that Allah gave the Qur'an to Muhammad on the 27th night of Ramadan. This night is called the Night of Power. It is a holy night. Many Muslims spend the entire night in prayer. Muslims believe that the angels pay special attention to people's prayers during the Night of Power.

Friday Prayer is performed every Friday at noon. Allah appointed Friday Prayer as a time of spiritual devotion and reflection.

Celebrating Today

Muslims eat their first meal before sunrise.

During Ramadan, Muslims begin their day before dawn. In some communities, bells are rung to remind Muslims to begin their first meal before sunrise. This meal is called the *suhoor*. When Ramadan falls in the winter, there are fewer daylight hours, so the suhoor is a smaller meal. In the summer, the suhoor is a much bigger meal. The Sun rises earlier and sets later, so Muslims must go longer without food or drink. They need a bigger meal so they have energy for the day.

After prayer, friends and family gather together for a festive meal. These meals are called *iftar*. The iftar meal is made up of many different kinds of foods, including vegetables, breads, meats, and desserts. The meal often lasts until the middle of the night. Many Muslims do not get much sleep during Ramadan.

DID YOU KNOW?

Muslims do not eat pork, bacon, ham, or any meat that comes from pigs.

Many Muslims break their fast by eating dates and drinking water. This is how Muhammad broke his fast 1,400 years ago.

Americans Celebrate

Ramadan celebrations are held across the United States every year. Special activities and public prayers in mosques are held across the country to show the American Muslim community's devotion to Allah.

The American Muslims Intent on Learning and Activism (AMILA) is a group that takes **spiritual retreats** in California every year during Ramadan. During these retreats, the group members study Islam and become closer to one another.

California

Many Muslims live in the United States. In 2001 the United States Postal Service honored the American Muslim community by creating an Eid postal stamp. The Eid stamp celebrates the Muslim festival of fast breaking. It was first released in Chicago, Illinois.

0   100   200   300 miles

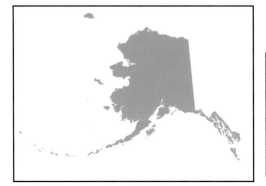

Once a year, Muslims in the United States and around the world donate to LIFE's Ramadan Food Basket organization. This organization gives food to poor families during Ramadan. The North American headquarters are in Southfield, Michigan.

Southfield Michigan

Detroit

New York

Chicago, Illinois

The number of Muslims in the United States is growing. New York state has the highest number of Muslims in the United States. Almost five percent of New York's population is Muslim. That means that about 100,000 people in New York celebrate Ramadan every year.

Detroit, Michigan, is home to the largest mosque in the United States. The Detroit Islamic Center has two floors. It can fit 1,000 people in the main prayer hall and more than 2,000 people in the banquet hall. More than 3,000 people could pray in the Detroit Islamic Center at the same time during Ramadan.

Holiday Symbols

Certain symbols remind people of Islam and Islamic festivals. These symbols are important because they represent different parts of Islam. Here are some examples of Ramadan symbols.

Crescent Moon

The crescent-shaped new moon signals the beginning and end of Ramadan. People climb rooftops and hills in order to see the Moon. In the United States, announcements are made on television and on the radio when the new moon has been spotted.

★ ★ ★ ★ ★ ★ ★ ★ ★

This Muslim mosque in New York City has a crescent-shaped sculpture. It is a symbol for the new moon.

The Qur'an

The holy book, the Qur'an, was given to Muhammad during the month of Ramadan. Muslims celebrate Ramadan and the Night of Power because of the gift of the Qur'an. Muslims believe their lives should be based on the lessons in the Qur'an.

Sunset and Sunrise

During Ramadan, the Sun controls when people can and cannot eat and drink. Muslims must eat and drink at night before the Sun rises and after it sets. In the Qur'an, it is written that you can eat and drink "until you can plainly distinguish a white thread from a black thread by the daylight." Try holding a black-colored thread and a white-colored thread outside at night. Is it possible to tell which is which?

Further Research

Many books and websites explain the history and traditions of Ramadan. These resources can help you learn more.

Websites

To learn about Ramadan, play games, and learn a new song, visit:
www.ramadankids.com

To find out more about Ramadan and the history of Islam, visit:
www.ramadan.co.uk

Books

Hoyt-Goldsmith, Diane. *Celebrating Ramadan*. New York: Holiday House, 2001.

Senker, Cath. *My Muslim Year. A Year of Religious Festivals*. London: Hodder Wayland, 2003.

Crafts and Recipes

Ramadan Calendar Chain

What you need:

Colored construction paper, glue, and scissors

Cut construction paper into strips 8 inches long. You will need 30 strips. Form a circle with the first strip, and glue the ends together. Then string a second strip through the first. Form a circle with the second strip, and glue the ends together. Keep adding circles until you have a chain of 30. Hang your chain on a wall. Carefully tear off one circle for every day in Ramadan.

Charity Decorated Jar

What you need:

Glass jar, glue, glitter, paper, scissors, and crayons

Ramadan is the time of year to remember the less fortunate. You can make a charity jar to keep coins that you want to donate to charity. Draw pictures of stars and the Moon. Carefully cut out the pictures. Cover the pictures with glue, and sprinkle them with glitter. Spread glue on the other side of the pictures. Paste them onto the jar. Put coins inside the jar.

Almond Cookies

Ingredients:
1 cup soft butter
1/2 cup sugar
1 teaspoon of vanilla
2 cups flour
whole almonds

Equipment:
cookie sheet   spoon
cookie cutters   rolling pin
large bowl

1. Ask an adult to turn the oven to 300° Fahrenheit.
2. In a large bowl, mix the butter and sugar together until it looks smooth.
3. Add the vanilla and flour to the bowl. Mix everything together with your hands.
4. Use a rolling pin to roll the dough flat. When the dough is about 1/4-inch thick, use cookie cutters to make shapes.
5. Press an almond into the center of each cookie.
6. Place the cookies on a cookie sheet, and ask an adult to put them in the oven.
7. Bake for 10 to 15 minutes or until golden brown.
8. Remove from the oven, let cool, and enjoy.

Holiday Quiz

What have you learned about Ramadan? See if you can answer the following questions. Check your answers on the next page.

1 What marks the beginning and end of Ramadan?

2 What happened on the Night of Power?

3 When can Muslims eat during Ramadan?

4 Who does not have to fast during Ramadan?

5 What did Muhammad eat to break his fast?

★ ★ ★ ★ ★ ★ ★ ★ ★ ★ ★

Camel races are an exciting part of the Eid al-Fitr celebrations in Saudi Arabia.

Fascinating Facts

★ Muslims try to read the Qur'an from start to finish at least once during Ramadan.

★ Muslims must always face in the direction of Mecca when praying. Muslims in the United States face east.

★ Before praying, Muslims wash the parts of their body that most often get dirty. These include the hands, mouth, face, ears, and feet.

★ There are more than 5 million Muslims living in the United States.

★ Many Muslim-American children attend Saturday school at a mosque or Islamic center.

Glossary

charity: giving money to the poor, sick, and needy

devotion: strong attachment and dedication to a religion

fast: not eating for long periods of time

miracle: an amazing event

pilgrimage: a journey to a holy place

prophet: a religious teacher thought to be inspired by Allah

recitation: saying aloud something learned from memory

revelations: messages from Allah

spiritual retreats: quiet places where people go to think about their religion

submission: obeying completely

Index